Doug

A Tale of Vampires, Maidens, and Stolen Candelabras

Shannon Mae

Blurb

DOUG

I have a problem—and it isn't just being a vampire named Doug. Maidens keep winding up at my castle, freaking out when they find out I'm a vampire, and stealing my candelabras. Really, it's enough to give a vamp a complex. Not to mention the fortune I'm spending on replacing the candelabras. Luckily, the nearby home store keeps them in stock. They also happen to employ a very cute cashier named Vlad, who ends up stopping by my castle. Now if I can only hide my fangs long enough to avoid him running off screaming into the night with my new candelabra.

`Vlad`

My mother was a fan of the supernatural (hence the name Vlad), but I don't believe the customer when he mutters about being a vampire (because what vampire is named Doug?). Imagine my surprise when I find out he really does live in a castle. Doug is a pretty extraordinary guy, and we have way more in common than I expected. Not only that, but things definitely seem a little fairy-tale-like, including how fast I'm falling for the cute guy who I just met. (And are those actually fangs in his mouth?)

Tags: Doug is tired of screaming maidens and stolen candelabras; Mrs. Butters is a meddlesome creature; Vlad really knows how to go with the flow, even if that means rocking a pink bathrobe; knitting and crocheting are art forms; flappy sky puppies are adorable.

Doug: A Tale of Vampires, Maidens, and Stolen Candelabras is a 16k short story.

Copyright © 2025 by Shannon Mae

All rights reserved. No part of this book may be reproduced in any form or by any electronic or mechanical means, including information storage and retrieval systems, without written permission from the author, except for the use of brief quotations in a book review.

NO AI/NO BOT.

We do not consent to any Artificial Intelligence (AI), generative AI, large language model, machine learning, chatbot, or other automated analysis, generative process, or replication program to reproduce, mimic, remix, summarize, or otherwise replicate any part of this creative work, via any means: print, graphic, sculpture, multimedia, audio, or other medium. We support the right of humans to control their artistic works. This is a work of fiction. Names, characters, places, and incidents either are the products of the author's imagination or are used fictitiously. Any resemblance to actual persons, living or dead, businesses, companies, events, or locales is entirely coincidental. The use of any real company and/or product names is for literary effect only. All other trademarks and copyrights are the property of their respective owners.

Editing by Shannon, Aspen Tree E.A.S.
Cover assembly by Tammy, Aspen Tree E.A.S.
Cover art by GrimmKat

Contents

Reader Warning	VI
Acknowledgements	VII
1. Chapter One	1
2. Chapter Two	13
3. Chapter Three	27
4. Chapter Four	38
5. Chapter Five	51
6. Chapter Six	62
7. Chapter Seven	75
8. Epilogue	88
Also by Shannon Mae	102
About Shannon Mae	105

Reader Warning

This book is intended for mature audiences. There are also some steamy times between men. All sex acts are completely consensual and fully enjoyed by everyone involved.

A Note Before You Begin

This book has been edited multiple times, but sometimes we miss something. If you notice a typo or grammatical error, please contact me! Sending it through Amazon is unfortunately not the easiest way to manage it. Feel free to email me at <u>authorshannonmae@gmail.com</u>. Thank you!

Acknowledgements

Thank you to my family and friends and all the usual crew - Maeflower, Scott, Tammy, Jennifer, Avril, Mona, Elizabeth, and everyone who provided support.

A special thank you to my Patreon subscribers, who encouraged me, helped with names, chose a title, and told me to include flappy sky puppies. I love you all!

Chapter One

Doug

The high-pitched shrieking was killing my ears. The maiden—I hadn't even gotten this one's name—was running down the staircase toward the great hall. I took a moment to marvel at her ability to run in those high heels—they had to be three inches and couldn't be much thicker than a dime. The blue ball gown she was wearing and her curly blonde hair were both flaring dramatically out behind her, and she was holding a candelabra in one hand. It looked like something out of a movie.

Only there was the screaming. Which was getting quite annoying.

"Excuse me, ma'am," I yelled.

She turned her head towards me while running, and I flinched, hoping she wouldn't fall. That would really complete the mess that was my life.

"Don't talk to me, you monster!" she screamed. Then she faced front again, all the while still running. She was almost to the bottom of the stairs.

"Do you think you could leave the candelabra? On the ledge by the main door? We only have one left..." I trailed off as the door banged open and then shut. "Or not. I guess now we have none left."

"Dear, was that screaming I heard?" Mrs. Butters asked, coming out of the kitchens into the great hall. "My, don't you look dashing standing there on the staircase in your dress pants and shirt—I'm guessing you were in a zoom meeting? Did you meet the lovely maiden who I let in earlier? Where is she?"

I sighed, rubbing my forehead. "Mrs. Butters, we've talked about this."

"My dear, what am I supposed to do? They come in from being lost in the forest, rain drenched, and they need a place to dry off and something to change into. You can't expect me to turn away poor, lost maidens," she announced.

"I'm beginning to think they just come here to steal fancy ball gowns and our candelabras. You know, that was the last one, and she took it with her," I told Mrs. Butters, walking down the stairs toward her.

She looked at me, disappointed. Mrs. Butters was like a grandmother to me—she had white hair, a full figure, and she always seemed to smell of cookies. She also did an excellent job at maternal disappointment. I tried not to disappoint her, seeing as how she basically ran the place. But... the maidens. I just couldn't take the maidens.

"That has to be the tenth one. At least," I complained.

"Dear boy, you're supposed to woo them. Dance with them, give them a feast, read books to them. What have I told you about showing your fangs the moment you see them? You've got to ease a potential partner into something like that," she said.

She produced, as if from thin air, a feather duster, and she bustled about cleaning the great hall.

"I didn't mean to show her... You know what, it doesn't even matter. I don't want a partner. And I'm not a boy. I'm ninety years old. I'm older than you," I mumbled, even though I knew I sounded like a petulant child.

"You have no idea how old I am. Besides, I'm sure ninety for a vampire is practically still a child. And you've collected dust in this castle for decades. It's time to get out and find love," she told me.

"No. It's time to get out and buy more candelabras," I said. Ugh. I hated taking a trip into town. It was far away, and it was all so... modern.

"Oh, I have a coupon for the home store in my bag. Let me grab it for you," she said, wandering off to go find her bag. "Get a bunch!" she called out.

I huffed out a breath. I took that to mean the maiden thing would continue to be a problem. I wondered if Mrs. Butters was somehow to blame. Did she take an ad out in the local paper? Free ball gowns at your local creepy castle in the middle of the woods? Really, I went decades without visitors, and now the damn maidens just wouldn't stop.

Mrs. Butters came back with the coupon—twenty percent off—and waved me out the door. I took the car, and about a quarter of a mile from the castle, it began pouring. Just great. Lucky for me, it only lasted about two miles, and then the skies cleared up, and it was sunny for the rest of the trip into town, which was not close by.

The home store was… awful. It was bright and loud, the aisles close together, with crap piled everywhere. Things had no rhyme or reason to them. There was a plush pink hairy-looking chair next to a golden gilded mirror, and next to that was some type of garishly modern looking end table with only three legs—it looked like it wouldn't hold a plant without toppling over.

Then there were the people. The place was packed. It was the middle of the day on a Tuesday, for goodness sake. Didn't these people work?

Yes, I was here, but I'm a ninety-year-old vampire who worked his ass off for years before my paternal grandfather decided to leave me a castle in the middle of nowhere along with an inheritance. And I did run a company. A small company, but enough to give me spending money so that the inheritance could go towards the upkeep of the castle.

You can not imagine how ridiculously expensive castles are.

Which brought me to the overstuffed, messy shelf that had the candelabras and other assorted candle holders.

Ugh, I'd forgotten it was October. There were candelabras with skulls, ones with snakes twined around the base, and ones with fake spiders attached. There was one with fake blood dripping off it, a garishly hideous pumpkin candelabra, and a rather creepy doll one.

I moved them around until I eventually found three plain black metal ones and a tarnished silver one that looked like a lovely antique. I hesitated at a raven candelabra, but Mrs. Butters, who'd worked at the castle for my grandfather, didn't like things to not match the "castle aesthetic," as she called it.

Yes, I knew it was technically my castle, but over the last two decades, Mrs. Butters had become my family, and I hated disappointing her.

Besides, some random maiden would probably just run off with the raven candelabra anyway, so there was no point in buying it. Although I guessed it could be worse—they weren't running off with books from the library (which I am rather fond of) or my yarn stash.

I carried my finds up to the line and waited behind a woman who looked like she was buying about thirty dishcloths. What could someone possibly need thirty dishcloths for? Ahead of her was someone whose cart was full of Christmas decorations. My god, it wasn't even November yet, and the Christmas decorations were out? I was glad I'd missed that section of the store. The thought of Christmas already? It was an abomination.

That reminded me of the maidens, who seemed to think I was the abomination. It was enough to give a guy a complex. So, I drank human blood to survive. It's not like I *killed* anyone. Most of the blood I drank came from a blood bank anyway. The modern age made being a vampire *so* much easier. Back when I was first turned, I actually had to *talk* to people in order to lure them off to feed. Of course, I made sure they were fine afterwards and got home ok. I wasn't a monster, despite what the shrieking maidens thought.

I was lost in thought when the old man behind me tapped me and said, "Register seven." Sure enough, cash register seven had a blinking light above it. I carried over the candelabras and placed them down, digging in my pocket for the coupon.

"I have a coupon," I started, before I heard a smooth, chocolatey voice welcome me to the home store. I looked up to see who the voice belonged to, but I was distracted by the guy's name tag. "Your name is Vlad? Are you kidding me?" I asked.

When I glanced at his face, my first thought was that he did *not* look like a Vlad. He had a total golden retriever vibe—he was smiling, and it wasn't even the fake *I work in retail and hate my life* smile. He had blond hair, he was wearing a *pink* shirt, and he even had dimples.

Fucking *dimples*. Like a ray of fucking sunshine.

"Yeah, my mom was super into vampires and the paranormal, so she named me after Vlad the Impaler, who was supposedly the inspiration for *Dracula*. She said she figured if she named me Dracula I would get bullied." He rolled his eyes at that. "As if Vlad wasn't enough for kids to make fun of."

"Try being a vampire named Doug," I mumbled under my breath.

Only Vlad the cashier heard me and laughed as he started ringing up candelabras. "Yeah, right. No vampire is named Doug."

I went back to digging for the coupon and pulled it out, handing it over. Vlad the cashier rang it up and told me the total—almost ninety dollars.

"Didn't it take twenty percent off?" I asked. Ninety dollars for candelabras that will run screaming out the front door was absurd.

"Yup. The coupon is only good for one item, though," he told me, and dammit if he didn't actually look regretful at the news.

At that moment Peggy walked by behind the counter, spotting me and the candelabras. "Ah. Is it the maidens again?" she asked.

I grimaced and nodded. Peggy was the assistant store manager, and she'd helped me find the candelabra section a few months ago. When they ran out on my third visit (or was it my fourth?), she promised to order more and keep them stocked. I don't think when she asked why I needed so many candelabras she believed my maidens-running-away-with-them story, but she treated it like an inside joke now.

"Give him twenty percent off the whole order, Vlad. He's a regular," she told him, typing something into the register, presumably to give me the discount. Then she turned to me. "Hopefully these last a few weeks! In the meantime, I'll be sure to order more stock."

Then she was off to help another cashier who was ringing up a disgruntled old man with a whole bunch of cat… things. Most of which were quite hideous. Apparently they really could sell anything at these places.

"Maidens?" Vlad the cashier asked as I handed over my credit card.

Since my entire existence was basically a comedy show at this point, I blurted out, "Yes. I'm a vampire who lives in a creepy castle in the woods and maidens keep popping up soaked and needing a change of clothes, and when they see my fangs they run off with a new gown and a candelabra."

He looked at my card and then me before ripping the receipt off and putting it in the bag with the candelabras. "A vampire named Doug?" He smiled at me and winked.

I just sighed, grabbed my bag, and speed walked out, ignoring what sounded like my name being called.

Fuck my immortal existence.

Chapter Two

Vlad

I leaned over the counter, yelling, "Sir! Excuse me, sir!" before I finally yelled out, "Doug!"

I was leaning so far that my feet were dangling, but there was no way I was hopping over the thing to chase down a customer. I barely had a moment to admire Doug's very fine ass in those black pants before he was gone.

He was *fast*. I could've walked all the way to the end of the string of registers to chase him down, but somehow at the pace he was moving, I doubted I'd catch him.

"Shoot," I muttered, holding Doug the not-vampire's credit card in my hand.

"What's up, pumpkin butt?" Peggy asked.

I couldn't help smiling before I held up the credit card in my hand to show her that the customer had left without it.

"Well, fuck a duck," she mumbled to me, taking the card and looking at it.

I loved my boss, which was probably why I still worked here. I've gotten pretty successful at my side gig, so that was really my main job now—I'm a voice actor, and in the last year I was finally making enough to pay the bills (and even go on a small vacation).

So why was I still working in retail? Recording audiobooks is a pretty lonely job, and I'm a social butterfly. Working in retail gave me a steady paycheck, health benefits, flexible hours, and enough people time that I didn't get too lonely.

And I got to meet people like not-vampire Doug, who really did have a fine ass. He was totally cute, all broody and dark-haired with that stubble, but his off-beat sense of humor was what really attracted me to him.

I was pan, and quirky was totally my type. A guy who came into a home store wearing dress pants, buying candelabras, and claiming to be a vampire with a maiden problem was right up my alley.

I snatched the card back from Peggy. "Maybe I can hunt him down," I said, still staring at the front doors where he'd disappeared.

"Vlad, you know store policy. We hold onto it in case the customer calls or returns for it," she said. "Besides, he'll probably be back in like two weeks. He only bought four candelabras. He must be repurposing them and reselling them or something, and that's why he doesn't tell us why he needs them. But it does remind me I gotta order more. You'd think the guy would just order from the internet by now, but…" she shrugged, as if she couldn't believe people still went to actual stores. Pretty funny considering she managed one of those actual stores.

Peggy started closing out my register then, and I looked at the time. Yup, my shift ended in ten minutes. Just enough time to bring my drawer to the back and count it down. I shoved the card in my pocket so I could stick it in the safe in the back room, grabbing the cash till and closing receipts from Peggy, who started walking towards the back of the store with me.

"So you don't think he's a vampire with a castle?" I asked, smiling at the guy's story again as we got to the back room door.

"Where the hell is there even a castle in Morningwood? We got Applebee's and Walmart, but last I checked, no castles," Peggy said.

A customer started calling out behind us, and Peggy ushered me in, closing the door and heading off to intercept the needy consumer. I walked over to the desk and saw Mel lounging in the chair next to it, chewing gum, and reading a book that looked like high fantasy. Mel was pretty awesome for a teenager—she was the definition of quirky. She was goth, or maybe emo? I didn't really know, but her aesthetic was all black with tons of cool silver jewelry, killer eye make-up, and chunky, kick-ass boots.

"Hey, Mel," I said, sitting at the desk and starting to sort the closing paperwork.

She popped a bubble, then looked up. "We live in one of the prettiest towns in the northeast for fall foliage, and I'm guessing Peggy's never made it out of the retail nightmare that's the center of town," she said, rolling her eyes. "We've got all sorts of weird shit around here."

I laughed. She was probably right, about both Peggy and the weird shit.

"Like what?" I asked, starting to count down the drawer.

"There's the abandoned railroad tracks. We've got caves, although none super deep or anything. The mill out on route seventeen looks like it could be straight out of a horror movie. Oh, and there's the abandoned asylum that's haunted. Quite the hangout spot, that one," she said, popping her gum again.

I stopped counting and looked over at her. "Mel, you really shouldn't be going into abandoned buildings with your friends."

She just rolled her eyes, and I got back to counting. I couldn't blame her—I'd done my fair of stupid shit when I was a teen too. I knew about the abandoned mill, and my friends and I had a rather infamous evening there with some liquor someone's older brother brought us.

"A castle, though. Don't think Morningwood has one of those. Nevermorn, on the other hand..." she trailed off, chewing her gum. I swear there was a smugness to that noisy chewing.

Nevermorn was the next town over, because someone thought it was cute to name the towns that way. As you could guess, there was a vicious, although mostly friendly, sports rivalry. The homecoming football game each year between towns was always packed.

"There's a castle in Nevermorn?" I asked, intrigued.

Mel shrugged. "Dunno. There's rumors, anyway." She popped another bubble, got up, and headed towards the door. "Have to start my soul-sucking shift with the zombies. Pray that my brains don't leak out my ears before the store closes."

I laughed as she left, then restarted counting the tens. I'd totally lost where I was, but a chat with Mel made leaving five minutes late worth it.

***

I ran a few errands before heading home. When I got there, I reached into my front pocket for my phone and realized that Doug's credit card was still in there. Well, fuck.

I *knew* I should give it back to the store, but it *was* late afternoon, and rush-hour traffic heading back toward work would suck. It's not like I could just hand it in tomorrow, either, because I was off for the next three days. What if not-vampire Doug came back before then?

Ok, maybe I really just wanted to see not-vampire Doug again. That stubble, those eyes, those sexy forearms—pair the package up with his quirky sense of humor, and I totally wanted to know more.

I tried to convince myself it wasn't creepy to google him. Of course the internet gods had his address listed, and when I put it into Maps, it looked like it wasn't that far off one of the state roads, although only the street name came up and not the number. It was definitely in one of the more densely wooded areas, though, so maybe that explained why. It wasn't too far from me, either. I wouldn't hit traffic going that way this time of day, and it *was* a pretty route to go admire the fall foliage.

Even though I knew it was a bad idea, I grabbed my keys and headed back out to the car, the directions still up on Maps. Maybe I could say it was on my way home? I could just, like, drop it off in the mailbox or whatever. Maybe with a little note and my phone number? You know, in case he had any questions?

Sure, that wasn't creepy. And it definitely wouldn't get me into trouble at work if not-vampire Doug was an asshole who reported me.

I just kept telling myself that as I drove, and I continued to tell myself that when Maps told me to make a left onto the road that Doug lived on. It was actually a really pretty spot, with the trees arching over it, even though it only appeared to be one lane. It looked like it would be a scenic drive, at least, even if I didn't find Doug's house.

I turned and drove down the road slowly, because I wasn't an idiot. I looked out for animals, too. I did *not* need to hit a deer.

When it started pouring, my face scrunched up and I put my wipers on high. I hadn't even noticed clouds when I left, and now it was like a freaking monsoon. I drove for probably another mile, and I was about to try and figure out how to make a U-turn on the narrow road, because the rain was pretty bad and I hadn't seen *any* houses yet, when my car died.

Because of course it did.

"Fucking hell," I mumbled.

I tried starting it a few times, but there wasn't even a sputter. I pulled out my phone and opened the internet to look for a local mechanic.

No service. Of course.

That wasn't totally uncommon when you drove west from town, but still. This was not my lucky day. The rain seemed like it was letting up a tiny bit, though, and I squinted out the front window. Was there light up ahead? Maybe the houses were just a bit further up the road?

I sighed, waited another five minutes, and checked the engine and my phone again. Nothing. I got out of the car and started walking.

"This is how horror movies start," I muttered, wrapping my arms around myself. I had a sweater on but no jacket, and I was quickly drenched as I trudged along. When I made it around a curve in the road, the rain stopped, and what I saw nearly took my breath away.

There was a castle.

DOUG

A fucking *castle*.

It was obviously not, like, a medieval European castle, but it looked like a damn good imitation. And there were lights shining from the windows, and it looked like it was positively glowing in the fading afternoon light.

I walked a little more quickly up the lane to the front door, shivering in my drenched clothes. Before I could even decide on knocking—was that a bat on the knocker?—the door was flung open, and a plump, white-haired older woman with an actual apron on was smiling grandly, saying, "Come in, come in! You must be soaked! We'll get you some dry clothes and..." she trailed off as she really noticed me.

"Hi," I said.

"You're not a maiden," she replied, looking me up and down.

"Ah, no, not a maiden," I said. "My car—"

"Yes, yes, it broke down up the road," she sighed. "Come in, then. Can't have you freezing to death on the grounds," she mumbled, ushering me in. "I don't suppose a ball gown will do for a change of clothes."

"Ugh, no. I don't usually wear ball gowns, although I bet I'd look great in one," I joked.

She looked at me sharply, and then she got this... I don't know, kind of gleam in her eye.

"You know, I never thought about it, but it would make sense, what with none of the maidens working..." she trailed off, looking me up and down again, then circling me like I was at auction.

I chuckled nervously. This was weird, even for me. This whole place was surreal. Was Tim Curry about to come down the steps in a corset? Had I fallen and hit my head on the road back there and this was all a hallucination?

"Alright then," she said, smile back in place as she practically dragged me down the hall. "Here's the bathroom. You get dried off. There's a robe on the back of the door, and you can make yourself at home in the parlor right over there," she gestured to a doorway across the large front hall. "The fire is already going, and I'll rustle you up some clothes."

"Well, I was actually just hoping to call a local mechanic—" I started, but I was pushed into the bathroom, the door firmly shut behind me. "And find out if someone named Doug lives here," I murmured to myself.

Because it was a castle. And the little old lady had been talking about maidens.

Poor Doug. I wondered if maybe he took care of his elderly grandmother or something, and she was delusional. I sighed and eyed the neatly folded towels on the bathroom counter and the plush robe hanging on the back of the door.

Might as well get dry, I figured, and began taking off my sopping clothing, pulling my phone, Doug's card, and my wallet out of my pants. I checked the phone again—I could just call the mechanic myself, or at least let someone know where I was—but there was still no service.

So weird.

Chapter Three

Doug

"...so I'm thinking a man-chest cover with some dark-haired guy, tons of muscles, of course, and maybe some blood dribbling down the side of his mouth? I haven't decided on a name for the main character yet, but I'm thinking maybe Rhys or Nyx?" Meg said.

"What about Doug?" I mumbled, scrolling through a photographer's website to look for what she wanted.

Meg laughed. "Doug! Oh my god, that's hysterical. Like a vampire would ever be named Doug!" She giggled a little more. "You are my favorite cover designer ever, though, so if you want a character named after you, I'm all for it. Maybe he can be the sweet best friend?"

I sighed. Always the side character, never the main character. That's what being a vampire named Doug got me in life.

"I'll send you over a couple choices," I said, clicking on a few models to email over. "You really want blood dripping from his mouth? I mean, you'd think a centuries-old vampire would have better eating etiquette than that. Do you really think they drool everywhere every time they eat?"

"Of course they do!" Meg insisted. "They're blood-starved monsters, you know. Can't control their urges and all. Besides, readers have to know it's a vampire book."

I just sighed again. Like someone who was centuries old wouldn't be able to control their urges. I had to resist rolling my eyes.

"You ok? You sound a little down," Meg asked.

"Yeah, I'm fine. It's just been one of those days," I answered.

I may never have met Meg in person, but I still thought of her as a good friend. I'd been making covers for her for years.

"What happened?" she asked, genuinely concerned.

"Really, nothing much. I guess I'm just feeling... I don't know, lonely or something. I'll be fine. It's just an off day," I answered.

"Another bad date?" she asked.

After the first few maiden episodes, when I *had* actually made an effort to be nice to them, I'd told Meg about them, talking like they were dates gone wrong. They kind of had felt like dates, although it had been decades since I'd dated. It had been disappointing that they'd all run screaming, but none of them had interested me much anyway.

"Yeah, I guess you could say that," I mumbled.

"Doug, can I be honest for a minute? You act like you're the problem, but maybe it's the people you're dating. I mean, it sounds like you aren't picking them, and maybe none of them are your type? Maybe you're looking for something different?"

"If I knew what I was looking for..." I trailed off.

"Well, maybe you need to make a personal connection with some girl or guy before you date. Maybe think about what you'd like in a partner," she suggested.

I hmm'd my agreement, thanked her for the advice, and we said our goodbyes.

I hung up the phone and stared off into space. She wasn't wrong about me thinking about what I'd like in a partner, although at this point, someone who didn't run off screaming when they saw my fangs was top of the list, and so far I'd struck out on that.

What really caught my attention was her casual mention of some "girl or guy." I had been born in a time and place where being straight seemed like the only option, but she'd just reminded me that we were living in different times. I'd had a few affairs when I was younger, but nothing serious or even terribly memorable. They'd been mainly with women, but there had been one or two male acquaintances. It wasn't unheard of for men to "help each other out," and I'd had a few of those experiences. I had chalked them up to youthful dalliances, because that's what the men had insisted they were.

I hadn't thought too much about any of it, with the men or the women. It was just an outlet, and I had other things to focus on when I was young. I was determined to work hard to build up my livelihood. Living forever meant paying bills forever, too. Fortunes didn't just amass overnight, and you couldn't be too blatant about anything or the humans got uneasy. No one wanted pitchforks and torches in the night.

Maybe I needed to… explore? Be more open-minded? Could I have gone ninety years of my life without ever considering that maybe I wasn't straight? Sure, I knew there were midlife sexual awakenings, but ninety seemed a little absurd, even if it wasn't really my mid-life yet. Was I really that dense about myself?

Mrs. Butters popped her head into the office. "Oh, good, you're done working!"

"Mrs. Butters, do you think I lack self-awareness?" I asked.

She actually laughed at me, like full-fledged guffawed. When she saw I was serious, she sobered up, though. "My dear boy, you're an artistic type, always getting lost in your art—we have rooms full of it to show that! You have a fine eye for artistic detail and what's beautiful, but you're not always the most aware of other things."

I blushed. "I wouldn't call what I do art," I muttered.

"Well, I most certainly would, so no more of that talk," she said. "Now stop wallowing and come down to the parlor for tea and scones."

With that, she was gone.

I shut down my computer, tidied up my desk, and got up to make my way down to the parlor. Maybe some tea and scones would cheer me up.

When I walked in, I absolutely did *not* expect the sight that met me. There was a man sitting on the old-fashioned red velvet settee, teacup in hand, looking toward the fire. He was wearing a plush pink bathrobe—probably one that Mrs. Butters stockpiled for the maidens—and I was captivated by the very male legs and feet that I could see peeking out from beneath the robe. It was a... distracting sight.

"Oh, it's you!" a warm, deep voice said, and I looked up to see a face I recognized. It was Vlad. From the home goods store.

"Ah, yes. It's me," I replied stupidly, still standing in the doorway.

"Well come and sit! Mrs. Butters made the most amazing tea, and I don't know what the hell this stuff is," he said, motioning to a jar of clotted cream, "but it is absolutely amazing on these... biscuit type thingies."

"Scones. And clotted cream," I answered, still staring.

Vlad was looking at me, his golden hair wet and mussed, his masculine hand holding the dainty teacup, and the furry pink robe extending over his arms as he leaned on the red settee. I was drawn again to looking at his legs, which were sprinkled with golden hair and led down to attractive feet.

It should have been absurd, but he looked adorable. And since when did I think feet were attractive?

He gestured for me to come into the room, so I did, sitting down on the dark leather chair opposite the settee. I reached forward to the little coffee table to grab a cup of tea and a scone.

"Very *Beauty and the Beast*," Vlad commented.

I stopped mid reach, staring at him. Did he think I was beastly? Already? He hadn't even seen my fangs yet!

"The whole set up, I mean," he said, gesturing around him. "Fireplace, dark leather chair, this dainty sofa thing, the whole castle and rain and all that. I mean, no wolves attacked me, but there's still time, right?" he chuckled. "I just came to return the credit card you left behind, but maybe I should ask if you're holding my father captive. I'm no Beauty, though, so..."

"I wouldn't say that," I mumbled, taking the credit card he pulled out of the robe pocket that I'd apparently forgotten at the store. I barely glanced at it, too busy staring at Vlad.

"Oh, you think I'm beautiful?" he said, batting his eyelashes playfully, and I swear to the gods that his eyes actually twinkled. I distracted myself by putting the card in my pocket and grabbing the teacup and a scone.

"You are," I finally said, because he really was, even in this ridiculous situation. "And you have a beautiful voice."

"I'm a voice actor, actually. I create audiobooks," he said.

I stared at him. "Do you really?"

"Yup. I love it. I just work at the home goods store to get some people time in. It's kind of lonely work recording audiobooks, although I do like dealing with the authors. At least most of the time." He grimaced at that last statement.

I laughed. "Tell me about it. I work as a cover designer, so I know all about dealing with authors."

"Oh my god! I wonder if we work for some of the same people! We have to compare notes!" he gushed.

We started chatting about authors and the writing community, and it turned out we did have some light overlap. He shared some rather hysterical stories (without names, of course) of the more difficult authors he'd worked with, and I did the same. We fell into easy conversation, drinking tea and snacking, and I barely noticed when Mrs. Butters bustled in to grab the tea tray and scones, leaving us to continue chatting.

By the time she came back and announced it was time to get ready for dinner, both Vlad and I were totally amazed to see that it had somehow gotten dark out. I didn't think I'd ever had such easy conversation with someone in my life.

"Well, dears, off with you. Time to dress for dinner," Mrs. Butters said, actually clapping her hands.

"I, uh, don't really…" Vlad started, but Mrs. Butters cut him off.

"You come with me, dear, and I'll get you all set. Go on, now, Doug, and get ready. Be in the dining room in half an hour," she ordered, and she dragged Vlad off, much to his bemusement.

I wandered off to my own room to freshen up. This felt oddly like a date, and rather than making me nervous, I was strangely excited. Vlad was funny and sweet, and we had so much in common.

Maybe I could manage to hide my fangs through the meal and have at least one entertaining dinner without someone running off and stealing a candelabra.

A vampire could always hope.

Chapter Four

Vlad

MRS. BUTTERS USHERED ME up an actual grand staircase to a bedroom. There was a huge canopied bed, plush carpets, white wooden end tables with candelabras on them (yes, they were the ones from the store this morning), and a giant wardrobe. And it was all shades of white and pale pink.

"Don't mind the color, dear. That can be changed easily enough," she told me.

"If the wardrobe starts talking, I'm just going to assume I hit my head and have a concussion," I said in reply.

She just looked at me oddly before bustling over to the wardrobe. She obviously wasn't a fan of *Beauty and the Beast*.

"Now, let me see here," she said, opening the wardrobe. I saw bright, frilly fabric, and she quickly shut the wardrobe door, giving a light, tinkling laugh. When she opened it again, there were pants and shirts in there.

"I swear I just saw..." I mumbled, but she just talked right over me.

"Now then, I think anything in here ought to be your size. You just help yourself. The bathroom is through there, so you can shower and get cleaned up before coming down to dinner. Any food allergies, dear?" she asked.

"Um, no," I answered.

"Well, hop to it, then!" she said, and she was out the door before I could ask any more questions.

I poked around in the wardrobe, and yes, everything was my size. Which was a little creepy. I grabbed a pair of slacks and a black sweater, opening drawers in the wardrobe to find socks and boxers as well. There were even shoes on the floor of the wardrobe, and I'd bet they were my size, too.

I left the clothes on the bed and headed into the bathroom to shower, because I did feel kind of gross after being caught in the rain. The bathroom was probably the size of my living room, and it had a huge tub with jets. I looked longingly at it, but I made my way to the walk-in shower to do a quick clean up instead. A half hour was not long to get ready.

As much as I wanted to luxuriate in the hot water—the products in here smelled amazing—I finished up quickly. I was really excited for dinner with Doug. He was a sweet guy, and we had a lot in common. I wasn't even sure if he was gay, but at the very least, I'd made a new friend out of this whole weird trip. I wrapped a plush towel around my waist and opened the bathroom door.

I stopped short the moment I stepped out of the bathroom. I turned and looked back inside. Yes, there was only one door, so I hadn't somehow gone into the wrong bedroom. I turned back around and took stock again. Canopied bed, yes. End tables with candelabras from the store, yes (although the candles in them were now lit, creating a soft glow). Large wardrobe, yes. My clothes laid out on the bed, also yes.

Pink and white frilly decorations? No.

The furniture was a dark wood color, the rug was a dark gray, the walls were a lighter gray (it actually looked really good, and I thought I might like it for my bedroom at home), and the bedspread was now a deep blue.

"What. The. Fuck."

I spun around. This was just… weird. I pulled my phone out again, and yup, still no service.

By the time I got dressed, I figured at least a half hour had passed. I grabbed a candelabra off the nightstand and opened the bedroom door. When in Rome…

The hallway still looked the same, and I figured I could find my way downstairs. Only Doug was waiting at the top of the stairs for me, and he looked…

Wow. Just... wow. He looked amazing.

He started to smile, and then he saw the candelabra in my hand, and his face turned... resigned? A little sad?

I walked over to him and held out the candelabra, forcing him to take it, although he looked perplexed. I stood back then, saying, "Wow. You look amazing. That suit fits you... just wow." I laughed a little self-consciously.

If he wasn't at all interested in me in a sexual way, I was probably about to find out, because there was no hiding my interest.

He blushed, though, still holding the candelabra tightly. "Thanks. You look amazing too. Like, really good."

I smiled at him and held my arm up, elbow out. "Shall we?" I asked.

He laughed and placed his hand on my arm so I could lead us down the stairs. It was all very old-fashioned romance movie, and my heart swooned a little.

DOUG

We joked with each other as we made our way to a fancy dining room with a large table, but the two place settings were at the head and second seat of the table, so we'd be close together. The table was already set with steaming platters of food, and it smelled absolutely divine. Meat and potatoes and vegetables, it looked like, and my stomach rumbled in hunger at the aroma.

Doug placed the candelabra quite far off to the side and well out of my reach, which was a little weird, but he obviously had some candelabra trauma in his background.

We both sat down, and we picked up our conversation right where we'd left off earlier, chatting like we'd known each other a million years as we heaped our plates full of food.

I couldn't help the groan that escaped my lips at the first bite, and Doug's eyes lingered on my lips. I licked them and watched his face.

Yeah, he was definitely interested. And the feeling was definitely mutual.

We talked and were flirty all through dinner, and Mrs. Butters bustled out the moment our forks were down to take our plates and bring out dessert—some decadently sweet coffee and a selection of mini cakes, including dark chocolate, cheesecake, and some kind of fruit thing that was to die for.

"You know," I commented, licking my fork just to see Doug's eyes flare, "I was thinking *Beauty and the Beast*, but maybe this is more *Hansel and Gretel*. Mrs. Butters doesn't have a really big oven, does she?"

Doug laughed. "I can assure you that Mrs. Butters is not trying to fatten us up in order to eat us."

"Yeah, I can't imagine her with ill intentions, because this is the best date I've had in... maybe forever," I said, watching to see Doug's reaction.

He smiled at me warmly, reaching out to grab my hand. I turned it over and laced my fingers through his. "Me too," he said. "My dating life has kind of sucked lately."

"She's definitely a good witch and not the evil kind," I joked.

Doug's hand squeezed mine, but then his eyes opened wide, and I swear it was like I saw something click in his brain.

He let go of my hand and turned his chair. "Mrs. Butters!" he yelled. "Get in here!"

Her voice preceded her arrival as she said, "Oh dear, he didn't run off with the candelabra, did he?"

When she walked through the door, she saw me and smiled. "Oh, good. You're still here. How lovely. Lately, the maidens don't even make it to dinner."

"Mrs. Butters," Doug ground out. I think he was clenching his teeth.

Uh oh. I think I just got Mrs. Butters in trouble.

Doug turned to me. "What *exactly* had you arriving here and appearing in a pink robe in the parlor?" he asked me.

I cleared my throat. "Well, when I saw you forgot your card, I might have looked you up online, and I thought maybe I'd just drop it in the mailbox or something. I hope that wasn't too forward of me."

His face softened. "I'm really glad you did, and I've really, *really* enjoyed our evening. I'm more curious about the pink robe, though."

"Yeah, I guess that's a bit odd," I chuckled. "Well, I was following the road, and there was a really bad rain storm—it literally came out of nowhere, because I didn't even think it was supposed to rain today—and my car broke down. I didn't have cell service, but I saw lights ahead, so I walked and found this place, which is amazing, by the way. Mrs. Butters greeted me at the door and told me to go dry off, because my clothes were soaked—"

"She greeted you at the door?" he asked, turning to stare at Mrs. Butters. She didn't look the least bit contrite, however. She was just smiling demurely by the kitchen door.

"Well, what should I have done, Doug? Left the poor thing in sopping wet clothes with no cell service and no car?" she asked sweetly.

"We *have* cell service, Mrs. Butters. We always have cell service. And we have a landline, too," Doug grumbled.

"Well, you two started chatting, and wasn't it the polite thing to do to invite him to dinner?" she asked.

"Mrs. Butters…" he growled warningly. "What did you do?"

I could tell Doug was getting really mad, and Mrs. Butters seemed to sense it too, because she went on the offensive.

"You're holed up here in this castle all alone, just you and your art, and it isn't enough. You need a companion, and you never go out, so really, what was the harm in bringing a few single people to the castle?" she asked, hands on hips. "You know, if you were more sociable, then this wouldn't even be a problem, but it's been *decades*, Doug, and you're lonely."

She was staring mulishly at him, her foot actually tapping. Doug growled at her... and I looked closer at his mouth, which was bared at her a bit like a dog when they growled.

"Are those... fangs?" I asked.

Doug and Mrs. Butters both immediately turned to face me. Mrs. Butters looked exasperated, and Doug looked disappointed. He leaned his head into one hand, waving at the front door with the other. "If you'll just leave the candelabra when you run screaming into the night, I'd appreciate it. I'm sure your car and cell phone will work just fine now."

Huh. I pulled out my phone, and yes, I did have full bars.

So weird.

"So, wait, you're *actually* a vampire?" I asked him. Then I looked at Mrs. Butters. "And you're, what, a witch or something?"

Mrs. Butters laughed nervously. "Well, I wouldn't say a witch, exactly..."

Doug looked at her too. "Are you serious? You're a witch? I've lived with you for twenty years, and you never told me that you had magic? What the hell, Mrs. Butters."

"Well really, dear, if you couldn't figure it out on your own, I wasn't going to fill you in," she harrumphed. "And you're one to talk. It took you *three years* to tell me you were a vampire, for goodness sake." She looked at me then. "Like I was supposed to believe the blood deliveries were because he had a rare genetic condition." She rolled her eyes.

"I still told you!" he yelled.

"No, I asked!" she yelled back.

"Children!" I shouted, because really, I didn't think this was going anywhere good when they'd devolved into a shouting match. They both turned to look at me rather sheepishly. "Perhaps you two can hash this out another time, when Doug isn't on a date?"

They both looked at me, shocked.

Mrs. Butters recovered first, smiling broadly. "Oh, of course, dear. I'll just leave you two alone, and head to my rooms, all the way on the other side of the castle, where I definitely won't disturb the two of you."

And with that, she bustled out the door and was gone.

Doug was still looking a little shell-shocked, so I picked up my fork and took another bite of the fruit thing. "This is *really* good. I wonder if it's magical, because if not, I'd love the recipe."

Chapter Five

Doug

Vlad was just... eating his fruit torte. Maybe he didn't actually believe me? Because he wasn't running screaming into the night. He wasn't even cowering in fear.

"I really am a vampire," I stated. "This isn't a prank. I'm sure you don't believe me..."

He stopped and looked up. "Do you know that your guest room was pink and frilly, but when I got out of the shower, it was all grays and blues? Trust me, I believe you. I know it's not a prank."

Then he went back to the fruit torte. Mrs. Butters could change the decorations? What the hell? Why had she made me paint my bedroom when I moved in? Why did I have to do any chores if she could just... magic stuff?

But that wasn't the point. Was Vlad just going to finish his torte and go? Was it actually a magical torte that kept him here?

"Do you feel compelled to stay? Maybe the fruit torte is magical..."

He licked his fork and looked at me, smiling a little. Yes, his tongue licking the cream was extremely sexy. No, I would not get distracted by that.

"I do feel compelled to stay, but only because I like you, Doug. And I grew up with a mom obsessed with vampires and supernatural creatures, so it's kind of cool to find out they're real. Plus, a lot of the myths are obviously wrong," he added.

"Yes, they absolutely are. We do *not* drool blood while we eat," I insisted. "Or kill people," I added. Because, yeah, I probably should have mentioned that first.

He just smiled. "You drink blood bags, so you don't need live donors. You can eat regular food. You're not a mind reader, and obviously you can't compel people if they keep stealing your candelabras. You can go out in the sunlight since you came to the store during the day, and you clearly weren't sparkling."

I snorted and rolled my eyes at the last one. Of all the ridiculous vampire stories to be told, that was probably one of the most annoying to me. I wasn't a unicorn that freaking sparkled in sunlight, for goodness sake.

Vlad continued, "You obviously don't turn into, like, a wolf or whatever—"

Only he stopped there, because he must have noticed my slightly embarrassed expression. And, yes, maybe I avoided meeting his eyes.

"Oh my god, you *do* turn into a wolf or something?" he asked, and he actually sounded giddy.

My face was warm, and I was sure I was blushing. "Well, you know, vampires usually come into some sort of supernatural skill…"

"Ohhh, let me see! Please!" Vlad asked, and he actually clapped his hands.

Fuck.

I did *not* turn into a wolf. My ability was not cute and friendly *or* ferocious. It wasn't really good for much, aside from the usual vampire jokes that got thrown my way over it. But if Vlad was going to leave, I might as well find out now.

I scooted my chair well back from the table, concentrated, and turned into my bat form. I was dark in color—black with some lighter gray throughout—and I looked like a typical bat, although I was larger. I hopped up onto the back of the chair and stared at Vlad, even showing my bat fangs and stretching my wings out. I waited for his reaction of disgust or horror or whatever, just hoping I had moved the candelabra far enough away that he wouldn't take it with him when he ran out.

"Oh. My. God," he pronounced slowly. "You're a bat."

I waited for the yelling or the freaking out.

Only his voice got soft and sweet. "Look at you, all fluffy and adorable with those big eyes and your little fangs!"

My fangs were not *little*, and I stared at him fiercely.

"Awww, you're so cute! You're like a flappy little sky puppy! So adorable!"

I am not cute, I spoke into his head. I was surprised I could even manage it—usually it only worked with other vampires or supernatural beings, and Vlad was definitely not supernatural.

Vlad gasped. "And you can talk in my head! That's so cool! Who wants a scratch? Do you want a little pet?" he cooed.

I am a creature of the night, bringing fear and despair, or at the very least disgust, to all who see me, I told him.

"You are *not* disgusting! You're adorable! I bet you feel as soft as you look. Who wants a little scritch behind their ears? Hmmm? Who wants a little pet?" he cooed again.

I stared at him, and he actually pursed his lips and made kissy noises at me. I hopped down onto the table, sure that my close vicinity to the food would gross him out. People generally did not like bats. We had a bad reputation and were often seen as bringers of disease and rodents of the sky.

Rather than being grossed out, though, he reached forward and started gently petting my head.

It felt... lovely.

"Aww, who's a cute little sky puppy? You are, that's who," he murmured.

Before I quite knew what had happened, I was cuddled up to him in bat form, and he was petting my head and back and even gently feeling my wings and oohing and aahing over how velvety soft I was.

I was getting into some kind of petting zen mode, and before I could embarrass myself by falling asleep in my bat form, I hopped back to my chair and changed back into my human form.

"Oh my god, that is *so cool*. You even have your same clothes on and everything. And your bat is so cute!" he gushed.

"Most people find bats rather creepy," I said, my face warm from the praise.

"Bats are extraordinary! They eat insects, including pesky mosquitoes, and they're pollinators. They look awesome flying through the sky, and some can even go up to sixty miles per hour! Echolocation is so cool, and did you know that they're the only flying mammals?" he asked. Then he laughed, adding, "Well, of course you know that."

"A fan of bats?" I asked, smiling.

"Oh, totally. I even have a bat house set up in my yard. I love going out at dusk and watching them fly around."

I just stared at Vlad. "I don't understand how none of this bothers you."

"Well, I told you my mom was obsessed with vampires. I always had... unique interests as a kid. I love fantasy and paranormal stuff. I think it's amazing that it's all real. Besides, I've had a few... interesting encounters over the years. I always kind of thought that there was more to the world than most people thought." He just shrugged after that.

"You're really not fazed at all by this, are you?" I asked again, mystified.

"Nope," he answered. "I think it's super cool." He laughed again, adding, "I really liked you *before* I knew all this, though. So don't think I'm just some fanboy hanging around because you have this vampire thing going on. Even before that, we had great conversations about our work, and I thought you were super cute and sexy the moment I waited on you in the store."

I blushed again. "I, uh, thought you were super cute, too. But I probably need to admit something..." I trailed off, unsure how to continue.

"Well, I know you're not married, because Mrs. Butters wouldn't be trying to get you a partner if that was the case. Unless there's a crazy wife hidden in the attic in true gothic style?" he asked.

I shook my head no, chuckling.

"And I already know you're a vampire and you can turn into a bat, so whatever you have to tell me can't be much more shocking than that." He leaned forward expectantly.

"Um, well... I've never actually... um..." I cleared my throat. Gods, this was awkward. I muttered, "I've never been with a man."

"What? You've never driven a van?" he asked, looking utterly confused.

Apparently muttering wasn't going to work.

I started to explain, hoping that would lessen the weirdness of it. "When I was younger, I was more focused on building up my portfolio and assets. Forever is a long time, and I wanted to be financially stable. I dated here and there, but more for the benefit of social norms than anything else..." I trailed off, unsure how to continue.

"Are you trying to tell me that you're a virgin?" Vlad asked.

"I am not a ninety-year-old virgin," I answered. "That would be a little extreme. I have had sex... I've just never, um, had sex with a man."

"Ohhh," Vlad said, leaning back and looking at me.

I cleared my throat again, feeling awkward and unsure.

"Are you attracted to me?" Vlad asked, and he didn't sound judgemental at all.

"Yes, very much so," I admitted, my voice getting husky. "I find you very sexy. I would like... Well, I'm not sure what I would like to do, never having done it, but you definitely appeal to me on every level. I would very much like to be intimate with you."

Vlad pinched his arm. I looked at him curiously.

"I must be dreaming. Not only do I meet a super hot and intelligent vampire who turns into a cute, flappy sky puppy, but he apparently just realized he likes men and wants to 'be intimate' with me. I must be dreaming, because this is too good to be true."

With that, Vlad got out of his chair, stepped towards mine, and pulled me up to standing. I stared into his eyes, waiting without breathing.

Was he going to kiss me? Oh, I really hoped he was going to kiss me.

Chapter Six

Vlad

I didn't think Doug was breathing.

He had been breathing—I was sure of it—but I was pretty sure he had just stopped. It was actually pretty awesome, because he looked totally fine and was staring into my eyes, blinking and everything and obviously not in distress.

I was planning on kissing him, but now I was just too curious.

"You don't have to breathe?" I asked.

Doug blushed—which made me wonder how that was possible if his heart didn't beat. Or maybe it did beat? But then wouldn't he need to breathe? Only he actually was breathing again now.

I pressed my hand against his chest, and yeah—he had a heartbeat.

"Uh, well..." he sort of trailed off, looking embarrassed.

"Doug, you turned into a flappy sky puppy in front of me. Nothing is going to freak me out," I reassured him.

"Well, we don't die very easily. Like, hardly at all. Even a stake through the heart won't do it. It's uncomfortable not to breathe or have a heartbeat or slow any essential bodily functions down, but we can do it." He sort of shrugged after that explanation.

"Were you not breathing because I have garlic breath?" I joked, only that made him blush even more.

"Oh my gosh, no! I was just... I just thought..." he trailed off, looking unsure.

I could tell he was getting awkward and self-conscious, which I absolutely did not want, so I leaned in and kissed him. He was so nervous it was adorable, and I just couldn't resist those lips another moment.

He was tentative at first, and I slid my hand from his chest around to his back, lightly resting it there. Our lips grazed against each other, gently exploring, our mouths slanting and parting a bit. I licked gently along the seam of his lips, and he opened up for me. I let my tongue flirt with his playfully.

I had every intention of taking things slowly, but my arms were suddenly full of sexy vampire, and he was frantically kissing me back. His hands were grabbing onto the back of my shirt, and he was rubbing against me, although I'm not even sure he was aware of it. I pulled him closer. I could feel his hardness against mine, and Doug was *definitely* on board with what we were doing.

I pulled away, both of us gasping for air.

"I don't want to rush you—" I started.

Doug cut me off. "I feel like I've been waiting my entire existence for this. Please don't make me wait any longer."

How could I say no to that? Doug grabbed my hand and pulled me to the staircase, practically running and dragging me with him. I wanted him more than anything, but I also *really* liked him. I hoped this wasn't just experimentation or a one-night stand to him. I mean, he was an immortal creature of the night, and I worked in retail and voice acting.

I didn't have long to worry about that, because Doug was pulling me into his room, and holy crap... There were candles everywhere. They cast a shimmering glow over the entire room, and it was utterly romantic.

Doug did not have the expected response, however.

"Mrs. Butters!!!!" he yelled, turning in a circle to look around his room.

I couldn't help it. I started laughing. I had a pretty good idea that the candles had not been here earlier.

If she could change the color of the walls and the contents of an entire wardrobe, I was sure setting up a few dozen candles had been pretty simple for her. Maybe she just twitched her nose or something.

"I think she's purposely not listening right now," I laughed.

Doug looked around, murmuring, "I can't believe her. This is so embarrassing."

I walked over, taking his face in my hands. "It's not embarrassing. It's romantic." Then I kissed him.

It was slow and sweet, and as our mouths tangled together, I had the thought that I could lose my heart to this sexy vampire. I knew it was too soon to think such thoughts, but it was like I had known him forever.

When our lips broke apart, I peeled my shirt off, and Doug did the same. He hesitated then, but I unbuttoned my pants and peeled them off, and though his hands went to his own pants, he sort of stalled out when my dick came into view. He didn't look nervous or hesitant, though. He looked... hungry.

DOUG

I pushed his hands away from his pants and he looked at me, blushing, because he'd been staring.

"It's ok. You can look all you want. You can touch if you want, too." I winked as I unbuttoned his pants and pushed them down along with his underwear. "Mmm, beautiful," I said as his dick came into view.

He blushed again, and I reached my hand towards his dick, looking at his face. "Ok?" I asked.

He nodded his head frantically. I gripped his cock in my hand, slowly jerking up and down, and he moaned as a little drop of precum formed at the tip. Holy shit, he was so sexy. I wanted to kneel down and take him in my mouth, but I also wanted to take this slow and savor every moment.

I stepped in and kissed him again, and I moved my hand until it was around both our dicks, jerking them together.

"Oh my god, that feels so good," he gasped between kisses.

"You're so sexy, Doug," I murmured back.

The pleasure was intense, but I wanted more. I pulled away and gently moved him toward the bed. He fell onto it on his back, his legs spread wide, his cock hard and red and jutting out. I leaned down and gave it a lick because I just couldn't help myself, and the sound Doug made—a moan that sounded like he was being tortured in the best way possible—only spurred me on. I took him in my mouth, working my tongue around the head.

"Oh my gods, Vlad. Oh my gods," he moaned.

I gently cupped his balls, and I slid my mouth down, taking him into my throat. His hips thrust up involuntarily, and he cried out at the sensation. Then his hands were on my shoulders, tugging me off of him and up onto the bed.

"You're going to make me come too soon," he gasped, and then he was kissing me frantically again, and I smiled against his mouth when we both took a breath.

"That's kind of the point," I joked, but Doug was shaking his head.

"I want a turn, too. But you have to tell me what you like," he replied, looking a little nervous.

I took his face in my hand and looked into his eyes. "I will love your hands or your mouth on me, but you don't have to do anything."

"I want to," he murmured.

He leaned in and kissed me, and then his mouth was traveling down my body. He kissed my neck, then down my chest, stopping at one nipple. He licked at it then sucked it into his mouth, his teeth grazing against it, and I shivered in pleasure. I felt his mouth smile against me, and he did it again.

"Fuck, Doug," I cried out. I imagined him biting me, and I felt my cock jump in response. Who knew that was such a sexy fucking idea? "You can bite," I gasped as he nipped at my nipple again.

I could feel him smile against me again, then his mouth continued to travel down, placing kisses and little nibbles against my stomach, then my hips. I tried to keep still, but fuck, I hoped he was headed where

I thought he was headed, but I also didn't want him doing anything he wasn't ready for.

"You don't have to—" I started, but then my dick was in his warm, wet mouth, and I gasped, unable to even finish what I was saying.

For someone who had never had a dick in their mouth before, Doug went at it with total and complete abandon, like a man who was starving and finally got a taste of food. His tongue was lapping at the underside of my cock and then at the slit as he moved his mouth up and down.

It was wet and sloppy and yet probably one of the best blowjobs I'd had, because Doug was moaning like he was getting off just by sucking on me. One of his hands was cupping my balls, and the other was jerking the shaft below his mouth, and holy shit I wasn't going to last. I felt like a fucking teenager.

"Shit, Doug, you're gonna make me come," I panted, trying to grab at his arm to pull him up.

Only me saying that made him moan even louder, and I swear he got even more frantic on my dick, his mouth and tongue and hands all working me over. I couldn't fucking take it. The pleasure was too intense, and the fact that Doug was so into it only made it hotter.

Another minute and I was groaning as I felt my orgasm crash into me. I had a moment of worry about Doug, but he moaned as I came in his mouth, swallowing down my cum as his pace got slower, drawing out my orgasm. Waves of pleasure rolled through me, and I was panting and quivering.

Then his mouth left my cock, his hand still holding me firmly, and I felt his teeth bite into my thigh. It was like the pleasure of my orgasm swept through me a second time, and I gasped and arched off the bed, feeling a gentle sucking on my thigh, Doug's hand lightly squeezing my cock.

I don't know if it lasted a minute or a year, but eventually Doug gave one final lick and came off my thigh, letting my cock go at the same moment.

"Holy shit," I murmured, and Doug laughed gently.

"Holy shit," I repeated. Because... wow.

Doug was sliding up the bed next to me, and he looked so fucking pleased with himself. I loved it. I pulled him onto me and leaned up to kiss him, even though I could feel him hesitate. Fuck that—he'd swallowed me down and sucked my blood, and I could sure as fuck kiss him. I moaned as I tasted myself on his tongue, and I felt his hard cock jutting into my thigh. He had obviously enjoyed himself, but I was going to make sure he got the same experience.

I reached my hand down, gently tugging on his cock as he moaned into my mouth.

"My turn," I murmured, and then I slid down and got him back into my mouth.

His dick was wet with precum, and I loved that blowing me had turned him on so much. It was sexy as fuck. I used every trick I knew, wanting nothing more than to make him feel good. When I swiped my tongue across the underside of his head and was rewarded with a spurt of precum, I moaned around him.

I wanted it all, and I sucked and licked and used my hands on him until he was moaning and writhing beneath me. When I took him into my throat and swallowed around the head, he groaned and thrust up, spilling into my throat. I pulled off a bit, wanting to taste him as he came. He tasted sweet, better than that fruit dessert, and I swallowed every drop.

When he was done, just lightly quivering, I leaned my head against his thigh, kissing it before I slid up the bed. He leaned in and kissed me, just as I had done to him.

We lay there, both of us panting, and I had a moment to wonder what came next. I was in this for the long haul, if at all possible, and I hoped Doug was too, but I didn't think after the guy had his first male sexual encounter was the time for that kind of conversation.

What did I do now? Cuddle? Get dressed and go? What did vampires expect after sex?

Better yet, what did Doug expect after sex?

Chapter Seven

Doug

Holy shit. I... Wow. I snuggled in next to Vlad, resting my head on his chest. I had a moment to wonder if that was weird. Was Vlad a cuddler? But he wrapped his arms around me and kissed the top of my head, so I figured it was ok. I traced my hands over his chest, and he squeezed me in a hug. It was sweet and comforting.

I had just had my first experience with a guy. I had just totally, completely, undoubtedly *loved* my first experience with a guy. I wondered when we would be able to do it again. I was a vampire, and I could go again without too much recovery time, but I was guessing Vlad probably needed a bit of a break. But the tastes of him—both his cum and his blood—were exquisite. I could live off his flavors. I didn't ever want to leave bed.

I almost laughed at myself. I was like a sex fiend—not ever a phrase I would have thought to use to describe myself. I was replaying it all in my head, enjoying the memory and feeling warm and comfortable, and I must have dozed off to sleep in Vlad's arms.

The next thing I knew, I was awake, and the bed was empty. I had a moment to worry that Vlad had left, because he could leave now if he wanted to, but then I heard a door open in the hallway.

Oh. Oh, no.

I jumped out of bed, ran out into the hallway, and yup, the door next to my room was open. It was an honest mistake—I guessed Vlad had been looking for a bathroom and didn't realize there was an en suite in my bedroom.

The door he'd opened was not another bathroom, however. Nor was it simply a guest room, or even my office. No, of course not. It was my craft room.

Well, one of my craft rooms.

My feet slowed to a trudge. Should I turn around and go pretend I was still sleeping? He'd already seen inside. If he was going to leave, best I just go curl up in bed and stay there forever. Or at least a year or two. I had plenty of time, after all. I could mope for a few years.

"Doug, get your sexy ass in here. I can hear you creeping out there," Vlad called.

I groaned a little and walked to the doorway, somehow hoping that maybe Mrs. Butters had done some magic and cleaned up the room and hidden my projects.

No such luck. It was just as much of a chaotic mess as always, and I cringed when I looked in.

Vlad was inside the room, holding a crocheted stuffed bat in his hands. The room was filled with bats. Knit bats, crocheted bats, bats made of paper, and hand-sewn bats. They ranged in size from one that was slightly bigger than me (that had taken quite a long time to knit, and a hell of a lot of stuffing) to one that was about the size of a thumbnail made from paper. There were floor-to-ceiling and wall-to-wall bats. Bats everywhere, with barely enough room to walk to the back of the room.

Vlad slowly turned to face me, and I cringed a little, realizing I was standing in my craft room totally naked. I hadn't gotten dressed in my panic, and now I felt exposed in every way. I grabbed a stuffed bat and held it awkwardly in front of myself.

"Did you make all these?" Vlad asked.

"Umm... Well, you know, when you live forever... It's quite a bit of time, really... Everyone needs a hobby..." I murmured.

Yes, I was a dork who made bats. The room was piled with bats, and this wasn't even the only room that was filled with them. Somewhere I even had some bat jewelry when I'd tried my hand at that—maybe the basement? Perhaps one of the other craft rooms? I couldn't even remember where that was stored.

And we wouldn't even talk about my attempt at painting. Drawing and painting were not in my skill set.

"Doug, you have a room full of flappy sky puppies," Vlad said, looking at the little crocheted bat in his hands. "My god, the detail on this thing. It's amazing."

Vlad looked over at me then, and he raised his eyebrows when he saw me. Yes, I was standing naked in my craft room with a stuffed bat hiding my dick, probably blushing because Vlad had happened upon my craft stash.

"Why, Doug, is that a bat in your pants, or are you just happy to see me?" Vlad smirked, walking over to me.

A laugh burst out of me, because damn, that was corny. Vlad walked up and cupped my face in his hands. "Are you shy about your art?" he asked, giving me a soft kiss before pulling back and waiting for an answer.

"Well, I wouldn't call it art..." I started.

"Doug, this is amazing. You have real talent. Do you sell them?" he asked.

"Well, no, I didn't think anyone would be interested in bats," I said. "It's just sort of a little hobby I picked up..."

"They're so detailed and beautiful. You're amazing," Vlad said, leaning forward and kissing me again. Our kiss was starting to get a little heated when I heard footsteps, and Vlad and I pulled apart to look at the doorway just as Mrs. Butters appeared.

"Mrs. Butters!" I cried, making sure the stuffed bat was covering me up.

"Psh," she muttered, "like I haven't seen it all before." Then she waved her hand, and Vlad and I both had silk robes on.

"Well, that's a nifty trick," Vlad murmured. "Really nice material, Mrs. Butters. Thank you."

I was still standing there sputtering, wondering what sort of magical creature Mrs. Butters even was, and Vlad was just pretending this was all perfectly normal.

"Doug, if you're done catching flies with that open mouth, you two can come down for breakfast. I've got quite the spread set up. Vlad, you'll have to tell me what your favorites are so I can stock them for nights you stay over," Mrs. Butters said.

"Oh, well, I don't know if he'd want to... That is..." I started, but I trailed off, and Mrs. Butters just shook her head and walked off.

I did want Vlad over again, but we hadn't talked about anything. We'd only met yesterday, as hard as that was to believe. Did Vlad even want a boyfriend? Did he want *me* as a boyfriend?

"Shall we go have breakfast?" Vlad asked.

When I nodded, he grabbed my hand and led me down the stairs to the dining room, which was set with a lavish breakfast.

"If the dishes start dancing and singing while we eat, you won't convince me this isn't an enchanted castle," Vlad murmured.

I laughed. "I had no idea Mrs. Butters was even... whatever she is."

Vlad looked at me, a half smile on his face. "I'm beginning to think you're a little clueless sometimes, Doug."

I raised my eyebrows. What did that mean?

Vlad just leaned forward and kissed me. "Let's talk over breakfast, my sexy vampire. I worked up an appetite, and we need to have energy for round two."

He winked at me and pulled me toward the table. I knew I probably had a stupid grin on my face, but I couldn't help it. I was definitely down for round two.

DOUG

We both ate, and we ended up talking about some of our favorite books. Any awkwardness quickly faded, and Vlad gave me a rundown of his coming week, which gave me a warm feeling. I was assuming he was telling me because he wanted to spend more time together, and I told him what I had on my agenda too.

I should probably just let things play out however they would. There was no rush, after all. I had eternity. I could see how things went, wait a few weeks or months, and then have the relationship talk with Vlad. There was no reason to rush things or put pressure on him. I certainly didn't want to chase him away or anything. Yes, I'd just enjoy whatever we were doing, no pressure and no stress.

"So, are we dating?" I blurted out, then I put my head in my hands.

I was so freaking awkward.

"Just ignore me," I mumbled into my hands, not looking at Vlad.

After a moment, I felt his hands on mine, pulling them away from my face. He was kneeling in front of my chair, and he was looking at me with the sweetest expression on his face.

"Yes, Doug, I want to date you. And it isn't because you're a vampire, or because you turn into an adorable flappy sky puppy, or because you're an incredibly talented creator who has a room full of awesome artistic bats," he said.

"It's not the only room filled with stuff," I mumbled.

Vlad smiled. "Well, then, you'll have to show me the rest later, because all of that stuff is pretty freaking awesome. It also isn't because you have some magical creature who can conjure up robes and redecorate your castle with a blink. Or the fact that you live in a freaking castle, because how cool is that?"

"I'm pretty wealthy," I blurted out, because again, awkward.

Vlad's grin got bigger. "It isn't because you're wealthy, either. Or the fact that the sex was fucking amazing, although it is definitely a relief that we're compatible in the bedroom, and I plan on heading back up there to find out more ways that we're compatible."

I blushed, but I also felt a wave of desire rush through me. Yes, I'd definitely like to end up back in the bedroom, too.

"I would love to date you, and all that stuff is icing on the cake. It's awesome. But before I knew any of that, I thought you were cute in the store. And once I was here, I felt like I was talking to my best friend when we were chatting. It was so easy and comfortable, and I feel like I've known you forever. I was hoping I wasn't just an experiment or something for you," Vlad said.

I looked at him, horrified. "Of course not! I wouldn't experiment on you!"

Vlad laughed. "I meant sexual exploration, because we're not in Frankenstein here, but I'm glad you want something long term. I'm hoping we end up being long term, because I really, *really* like you, Doug."

"I really, *really* like you too, Vlad," I said, and this time I leaned forward to kiss him.

When Vlad took my hand and we both stood up, I knew we were headed back to the bedroom, because we were both hard and horny. My heart was full, too, because I felt like I had finally found someone to connect with. Someone who saw me for me, and who liked what they saw.

As we walked out of the dining room, I cast a glance back and saw the candelabra sitting on the table.

"I might need to come up with an excuse to visit you at work," I said as we walked toward the stairs. "I don't think there will be any more maidens running off with my candelabras."

"I'm not a maiden, and I'm definitely not running off. The only place I'm running is to your bedroom," Vlad joked.

With that, we did run up the stairs, and we landed on my bed in a pile of out of breath laughter. It wasn't long before we were kissing and stripping off the robes

Mrs. Butters had somehow conjured for us. I looked forward to a morning of tasting and touching and exploring, and I couldn't help the smile that wouldn't leave my face.

Maybe Vlad was right and we were in a fairy tale, because I felt like this was the beginning of my happily ever after.

Epilogue

Vlad

"What on earth do you need all those for?" my former manager asked me. "It's kind of a crazy order. And to gift wrap all that..."

I just smiled at her, and she rolled her eyes. I'd gotten Doug other stuff to commemorate the anniversary of our first date, but I thought he would appreciate this gift the most.

I'd quit working at the home goods store a few months after I'd met Doug, because my voice acting work had picked up enough that it took most of my time. I still kept in contact with everyone at my old job, though. I was a people person, and I liked being the one to run errands. Doug was more of an introvert, and he got enough peopling by helping his clients and talking to them.

I left the store and climbed into the car to head to a local craft fair, excited to see Doug even though I'd just seen him that morning. A few months after we started dating, Doug had asked me to move in with him. It hadn't come as a shock, since Mrs. Butters had been hinting at it for weeks before that. Doug had blushed every time she not so subtly talked about how much easier it would be if I lived there.

I was pretty much living there at that point by then anyway, so it was really only a matter of making it official. Doug was very cautious of moving too fast, but I adored the man, and I'd made him very aware of that fact. I wasn't shy about telling him I loved him, and he wasn't shy about telling me right back.

It was all incredibly sweet, and I often still joked that I'd fallen into a fairy tale.

Of course, we had our fair share of disagreements. The biggest one had to do with knit bats, of all things. He'd cleared out the room next to our bedroom and made it sound proof so I could work there. It was incredibly sweet, but I'd also sort of flipped out, because where had all the bats gone?

I ended up yelling at Doug about how incredibly talented he was, and that we were either going to decorate the entire castle with bats, because we weren't shoving them in random rooms anymore, or we were going to start an online shop and sell them. He'd been mad that he did all that work for my office and I wasn't excited (Mrs. Butters hadn't helped), and after a bit of yelling about how talented we each thought the other person was, we'd discussed it like rational adults.

We'd had great make-up sex afterwards, too.

I pulled into a parking spot—the lot was packed, which boded well for business. It was a nice afternoon, and the place was bustling. When I made it to Doug's booth, I wasn't surprised that it had lots of people looking around. Bats were popular. Doug still seemed shocked by that, but I wasn't. We'd even expanded into t-shirt printing, but the handmade knit and crochet bats were still the bestsellers. We sold most of our items online, but we did a fair business at local events too.

Everyone was always amazed at how much inventory Doug had, and they thought he must craft all day and night. I didn't tell them this was decades worth of work, but I chuckled every time someone commented.

"Vlad!" Doug cried when he spotted me.

I walked over and gave him a kiss. "Hey, flappy sky puppy," I murmured against his lips.

He chuckled lightly. Somehow, it had become a term of endearment, and I loved teasing him with it. I was still amazed every time he turned into a bat for me, and he was adorable as a flappy sky puppy.

I kind of hoped I'd get the same ability. All vampires apparently had something, and I could think of nothing cooler than flying around with Doug.

Because, yes, I was going to become a vampire. How freaking cool was that? I think Doug was more nervous about it than I was, because he was afraid I would regret my choice and regret "being stuck with him forever" (his words, not mine). He was also afraid that something would happen to me and I'd die if I didn't become a vampire, although Mrs. Butters had assured him that we had a few years—at least—to decide.

Neither of us were sure exactly what that meant. Had she cast some sort of protection over me? Could she see the future? We didn't know.

We still weren't sure what kind of creature she was. We had made a game of guessing, although we kept those guesses to ourselves now. When we had jokingly asked if she was a house elf, she had gone off on a tirade about house elves not even being real supernatural creatures and "that woman," and we'd decided since then to keep our mouths shut.

Mrs. Butters was feisty when she was mad.

Besides, it was kind of fun not knowing what she was.

"Brownie," I said as I sat down.

Doug knew I wasn't talking about the delicious chocolate treats, and he looked thoughtful. He totaled someone's purchase and took payment, and I waited while he made small talk.

When they left, he said, "That could work. I was kind of thinking fae, though."

"Because of the food?" I asked. Mrs. Butters was the most amazing chef ever, and although I didn't think that was necessarily a fae trait, the food being somehow enchanted did make sense.

"Yeah, and the ability to change things around, like a glamour," Doug answered.

"Hmmm, yeah, I think that's possible," I said.

"I like brownie, too, because I don't think fae are really housekeepers. Maybe she's half and half," he said.

I had a chuckle over that—I wasn't sure fae and brownies would mate, but having no actual idea about either one, I couldn't say.

"Good business today?" I asked, although I already knew the answer. I'd helped him pack up the merchandise, after all, and there was quite a bit missing from his booth.

"Yeah, and I even got two commissions, so that's pretty exciting," he answered.

"Awesome! That's great! I'm so proud of you!" I said.

Doug turned red at the praise, but I *was* proud of him. He worked hard, he was creative as hell, and he'd turned his hobby into a profitable business. It was pretty awesome.

The craft fair was nearing its closing time, and I could tell people were starting to head out, but a big guy came into the booth—he had a beard and shaggy hair, and although he was tall as hell and looked really strong, he also had a dad bod. He was like the personification of a bear, and he was pretty sexy.

"Sas," Doug said, nodding his head in greeting. Obviously he knew this guy, but he was looking at him with some level of... I didn't even know. Distrust? Annoyance?

"Toothless," the guy responded.

Doug frowned at that and folded his arms, which just made the big guy laugh.

I was super curious, but I refrained from asking questions. I knew Doug didn't have any male exes, because I had been his first boyfriend, but there was obviously some history here. The guy stood aside as the last two people in the booth came over to check out, and Doug made small talk with them as he totaled up their purchases.

"You know, I'd heard it, but I wasn't sure I believed it," the guy said to me. He was next to me, which startled me. For such a big guy, he was quiet as hell. I swear he'd still been over at the entrance to the booth.

"Heard what?" I asked.

"That Doug had settled down and found a mate. Good for him. I'm really happy for you two," he said.

I looked at him, and he finally stuck out a hand in greeting.

"I'm Fred," he said.

"Vlad," I answered, shaking his hand.

He looked surprised, and then he burst into laughter again. "Vlad, huh? Well, isn't that just perfect." He shook his head, obviously amused, although I had no idea why. "Doug and I crossed paths ages ago on some business, and I like to keep track of people I've worked with. I heard through the grapevine that he's settled down, and I figured I'd stop in and say hi."

Doug walked over at that moment, since the last shoppers were done and the booth was empty.

"Interested in some stuffed bats?" he asked Fred. He still looked slightly aggravated.

"Aw, you're not still holding that wendigo incident against me, are you?" Fred asked.

Doug sniffed. "I could have died."

"Only, you know, you can't die," Fred replied, smiling.

"I could have been dismembered and partly eaten, and that's just... no thanks," Doug retorted, making a sour face.

"I said I was sorry," Fred answered, and he had big, sweet puppy-dog eyes as he stared at Doug.

I'm not sure how he remained unmoved by that face, but Doug looked at me. "Don't fall for his shit. One moment you're drinking beer at a tavern, and the next you're bait for a wendigo."

I burst out in laughter. "That sounds like a story I need to hear."

Doug sighed, then turned to Fred. "I guess you can come over for dinner. Mrs. Butters always makes plenty of food, and she probably somehow knows I'll have a guest anyway."

Fred looked thrilled. "Great! I'll see you at your place in an hour or so!" And he turned and walked out of the booth.

Doug sighed, and then he started gathering stuff to pack it up. I helped, looking over at him curiously.

"Fred probably knows my address. He's... I don't know, a bounty hunter of sorts. Something like that.

He never quite answered that question when we met," Doug explained.

"Why'd you call him Sas?" I asked.

"Oh, because he's a sasquatch," Doug said, like that was a perfectly normal thing to say.

I paused in loading up a storage container. "Are you serious?"

"Yup. He's also a pain in the ass," Doug grumbled.

"You think everyone is a pain in the ass," I laughed.

He came over and kissed me. "Everyone but you, Vlad. Everyone but you."

My heart melted a little, and yeah, maybe we stopped packing up to have a make out session.

We still managed to pack up and load the cars quickly, and I followed Doug home. We decided to leave unpacking the cars for after dinner, since we figured Fred would probably be arriving soon.

When we walked inside, there were boxes of various sizes stacked in the entryway. Twelve of them, to be exact. Doug looked surprised at the chaos.

"Happy anniversary!" I said, grinning at him.

He looked at me and smiled, laughing. "I was hoping to surprise you later with something, but of course you wouldn't have forgotten."

He came over, hugging me. I kissed his head, rubbing his back.

"How could I possibly forget the day I met you?" I asked. "Now open them up!"

"Fine, but I'm still saving my gifts for you for after dinner when Fred's gone."

"Ohhh, that sounds fun," I said, winking.

"Get your mind out of the gutter," he laughed, tearing open one of the boxes. He peeked inside, sputtered, and looked at me.

I couldn't help the huge grin on my face or the laugh that escaped at his expression. He pulled a large, ornate candelabra out of the box. It was a beautiful and fancy one. He put it on the ground and opened another box, his disbelief growing as he pulled another candelabra out. This one was made to look like bat wings, and it had great artistry. He pulled open another box, pulling out a campy, Halloween candelabra. He was tearing through the boxes now, making noises of disbelief as he pulled out all twelve candelabras.

When they were all lined up in the front hall, a jumble of empty boxes sitting off to the side, he walked over to me, leaned up, and kissed me softly, our lips brushing together.

"You'll never need to worry about disappearing candelabras again," I murmured, "or screaming maidens. I'm so thankful for you and for this past year with you."

"I'm thankful everyday for Mrs. Butters being meddlesome, and for forgetting my credit card," Doug replied, resting our foreheads together. "I love you, Vlad."

"I love you, too," I said, reaching to cup his face and then pressing our lips together again.

I couldn't wait to get Doug alone later, but that could wait. We had eternity, after all. In the meantime, I was looking forward to our housekeeper of unknown supernatural origin making us some excellent food and hearing some crazy stories from a sasquatch named Fred.

I was living a fairy tale, but it wasn't because of all the supernatural creatures that existed. It wasn't because Doug drank blood and would live forever, or because Mrs. Butters could conjure up clothes (among other things), or because we were about to have dinner with a sasquatch. No, the fairy tale was evenings cuddling on the couch, kisses in front hallways, and waking up in the same bed as Doug every morning.

Sometimes the ordinary things were what made life truly extraordinary.

Also by Shannon Mae

**Demonic Disasters and Afterlife Adventures:
(Paranormal Romance)**

A Beginner's Guide to Death, Demons, and Other Afterlife Disasters

A Beginner's Guide to Mistakenly Summoned Demons and Other Misadventures

A Beginner's Guide to the Care and Feeding of Demons (A Novella)

A Beginner's Guide to Revenge, Chaos, and Other Absurd Escapades

A Beginner's Guide to Demonic Possessions (A Novella)

A Beginner's Guide to Christmas Miracles (A Holiday Novella)

Collections:

Demonic Disasters and Afterlife Adventures Collection 1

Hellhounds of Paradise Falls: (Paranormal Romance)

How to Flirt with a Hellhound

How to Hack a Hellhound

How to Tame a Hellhound

Tinsel and Tentacles 2.0: Written with Amy Bellows

(Paranormal Holiday Romance)

A Merry Christmas for Art... and His Tentacles

SHANNON MAE

German Translations

Tod, Dämonen und andere Jenseitskatastrophen – ein Leitfaden

About Shannon Mae

Shannon Mae began her journey in the M/M romance world as an avid reader, then a beta reader, and eventually an editor who works with the unparalleled Tammy B. PA from Aspen Tree E.A.S.

When a dear friend suggested she should write her own book, she decided to do just that. She gravitates to writing paranormal romance, since that genre is her first love, and her books tend to be low-angst and filled with happily-ever-afters.

She is an unfailing optimist with a side of snark and sarcasm. When she isn't editing, writing, or working her day job, which she loves, you'll find her on some outdoor adventure or embarking on a hands-on project (that is probably slightly more complex than she thought it was).

She lives in a small, seaside town on the east coast, and she spends her free time with her eye-rolling, sassy teenage daughter and her adorably loving dog.

Life is a place full of mysteries and wonders, and she hopes to capture that joy and fun in her writing. Adding some fun, sexy times makes it all complete.

Shannon Mae loves hearing from readers!

Join for updates and all kinds of fun things!

Visit Shannon's website www.shannonmae.com and sign up for her newsletter! You'll get teasers, free chapters, and all the latest updates!

Instagram – https://instagram.com/shannonmaemm?igshid=YmMyMTA2M2Y=

Amazon Author Page - amazon.com/author/shannonmae

Facebook - https://www.facebook.com/profile.php?id=100090405068101&mibextid=LQQJ4d

Printed in Great Britain
by Amazon